BECAUSE YOU ARE MY TEACHER

By Sherry North · Illustrated by Marcellus Hall

Abrams Books for Young Readers, New York

This book features two of Earth's five oceans and all seven of its continents. The five oceans are the Arctic, Atlantic, Indian, Pacific, and Southern. The seven continents are Africa, Antarctica, Asia, Australia, Europe, North America, and South America. Blue whales live in all of the world's oceans, including the North Atlantic; camels and Egyptian pyramids are in Africa; penguins live in Antarctica; howler monkeys and the Amazon River are in South America; the Great Wall of China is in Asia; the deepest, darkest ocean is the Pacific; African elephants live in the grasslands and forests of Africa; the Grand Canyon (in the state of Arizona) is in North America; kangaroos live in Australia; the Everglades (in the state of Florida) are in North America; and the city of Venice (in the country of Italy) is in Europe.

The illustrations in this book
were created using watercolor on paper.

Cataloging-in-Publication Data has been applied for
and may be obtained from the Library of Congress.

ISBN 978-1-4197-0385-0

Text copyright © 2012 Sherry North
Illustrations copyright © 2012 Marcellus Hall

Book design by Chad W. Beckerman

Printed and bound in China
10 9 8 7 6 5 4 3 2 1

ABRAMS
THE ART OF BOOKS SINCE 1949
115 West 18th Street
New York, NY 10011
www.abramsbooks.com

For my parents, who taught me to
reach for the stars, and for the teachers
who showed me how
—SN

If we had a schooner, we would have our class at sea

And study the Atlantic, where the great blue whales roam free.

If we had some camels, we would trek through desert lands

To see the ancient pyramids rising from the sands.

If we had a chopper, we would soar above the cone

Of a rumbling volcano as it churns out liquid stone.

If we had sleek ski gear, we would cross Antarctic fields

To find the spot where penguin chicks are eating their first meals.

If we had a river raft, we would tour the Amazon

And listen as the howler monkeys growl their spooky song.

If we had hot-air balloons, we would set out on a quest

To study China's Great Wall from the east end to the west.

If we had a submarine, we would see amazing sights

In the deepest, darkest ocean, where the fish make their own lights.

If we had an off-road truck, we would ride savanna trails,

Where Africa's young elephants hold on to mothers' tails.

If we had swift kayaks, we would plunge through twists and falls, Exploring the Grand Canyon, where the river carves the walls.

If we had hang gliders, we would get a bird's-eye view

Of the Australian outback and the large red kangaroo.

If we had an airboat, we would roam the Everglades,

Where alligators stalk their prey, and lizards change their shades.

If we had a gondola, we would glide beneath the stars

In Venice, where the people ride in boats instead of cars.

If we had a rocket, we would study Earth from space.

With seven sprawling continents, our home is quite a place!

Our classroom is our vessel,

always headed someplace new.

Because you are our teacher,

We'll explore the world with you.